Barking at Windmills

Words Are Dogs Barking at Windmills

Michelangelo

VANTAGE PRESS
New York

FIRST EDITION

Published by Vantage Press, Inc.
516 West 34th Street, New York, New York 10001

Manufactured in the United States of America
ISBN: 0-533-12586-3

Library of Congress Catalog Card No.: 97-91162

0 9 8 7 6 5 4 3 2 1

To my friend, Chucky Pine Cone Seed,
may your forest be a chorus

Contents

Words Are Dogs
Barking at Windmills

Poem I

Where
Can a man
Find
Courage
When
He
Does
Not know
His own heart
How
Cruel are
Treasures
To the man who loves
Everything
How
Generous is
Poverty
To the man who loves
Only
Love

Poem II

The Alchemist's
Secret
Lies
In his ability
To turn
Lead into gold
Faced
With this
It seems
Little to ask
To transform this thorn into a rose
But
Alas
The petals remain dry
And the stem
Sharp
Your   softflesh
Gives
Way
To my
            selfish
Will
Blood
comes

Poem III

The Man gazed upon what was beautiful
Without seeing what is Absolute Beauty
The Woman spoke of what was lovely
Without speaking of Absolute Love
How can I only hold the Child
Without sensing the Absolute Union of manwoman

Poem IV

Love maimed
Socrates proclaimed,
"There is no wisdom in opinions."

Poem V

I turn from this world
And I look into the Abyss
Simply by closing my eyes
I know that it frightens me and I leave
With the effort of parting my lashes

I turn from this world
And I enter into the Abyss
Simply by pressing on her flesh
I know that it frightens me and I leave
With the effort of tightening my muscles

Poem VI

Who is ever really solitary in this world
Who is ever not
The Yin Yang are eternally joined
And infinitely separate
Has human Love done more to Destroy
Than Hate has to Unite
What is Divine has no boundaries
No difference
For where boundaries exist Harmony is divided
And therefore
Cannot be true
There is no thin line between you and me

Poem VII

When are man and woman ever closer
When they are joined in flesh or heart or both
Manfleshwoman
Manheartwoman
Manwoman

Poem VIII

Sung by the beaks of birds are your words blowing in
the day's breeze
Your goodness is in the flowers
Your kindness in the trees
I hope for understanding
But understanding does not come
I think how much like this stump my heart has become
I see the Beauty of Your hand
And yet, I feel forgotten
I cannot enjoy how You work through Man
Just one leaf of autumn

Poem IX

If
I
Could
Say
What
I want
To
Say
It
Would
Be
That
When
I
Kneel
To
Pray
I cry
    tears
        fall
            down
                from
                    my
                        eyes

Poem X

Words
Spoken truly
Come
Without
Anticipation
Prayer
Is
Not planned
It flashes through our core
We see
It
After
Not
Before
Only the Desert
Knows
The
Circumference
Of
The Oasis

Poem XI

White clouds spread and rise
Dancing steps against blue skies

Yesterday I thought I was wise
Today I am dumb
A mother lost her son

Who am I to try and realize
With a handshake of condolence another's love ties
Tears are all that are clear in the father's eyes

Yesterday I thought I was wise
Today I am dumb
A mother lost her son

Tonight the Moon hangs high
Tomorrow the Sun will rise
Dancing steps against blue skies

Yesterday I thought I was wise
Today I am dumb
A mother lost her son

Brendan Foley, in memory of 12/9/96

Poem XII

What did I know of the snare
To come from so simple a stare

Poem XIII

I believe
That we
Meet
For
Many reasons
That
Someday
Become
One

Poem XIV

I am dancing with two women
Oh what a clown I must appear
The women all sneer
The men seem to like it
They cheer
And cheer
And cheer
"Buy that guy a beer!"
They cry
"Buy that guy a beer!"
They wouldn't understand if I denied
"I don't drink beer, I fear."
So I drink it all up
Bottoms up with all the bubbles
I turn back to my partners
I the only one seeing double?
I am dancing with two women
A Lover, and a Friend
But when I look into their eyes they both regard me the
same way

Poem XV

I
Have
Destroyed
A
Heart
When
I
Do
Not
Know
My own
And still
Every instinct
Moved me
To
Depart
Like
Wind
Under
The
Closing window
No man should have such power

Poem XVI

Rejoice in your voice

Poem XVII

Tragedy is Beauty remembered
Wrinkles lay across her cheeks like plowed furrows on a
    bed of youth

Where have all the children gone?
Following the Piper's perfect promise
No more trampled flowers in my garden

No tighter cell than a despairing mind in a young body
No wider space than a young mind in an old body
I take no issue anymore except with myself

Tragedy is Beauty remembered
But Beauty possessed and ignored is truly to die

Poem XVIII

Do
Not
Tell
Me
That you
Cannot
Live
Without
Me
For
I
Will show you
That this
Is
Not
True
Carried off by
The
Same
Silver breeze
That
First
Lifted me
To
Your
Lips
I am no now than that first night
heavier
And
The Wind
With
White

Words
Whispers
It
Will
Be
Held
Nay
By
Your golden box
Nay
Your golden locks

Poem XIX

There once were two trees who could not see each other
clearly
Anymore
For the Wind was blowing across the pond water at
their feet
Making the Water shiver where it once was still
The Wind seeing how sad he had made his friends
Tried to help by blowing harder
Bending them down to see one another
More clearly in the pond
Yet, the harder
That the Wind blew
The more his sister the Water
Shivered
And the harder
That the Wind blew
He heard the branches and the trunks of the Trees
crying
"Wind, if you bend us closer to the Water we will break
and die!
For our roots are selfish and laugh at us as they cling to
the warm earth.
They are content
Where they are
And are too frightened to meet you Wind.
They will not move even if it means we shall break and
perish.
Our roots are so selfish
So please,
Wind stop blowing."
To this the Wind replied
"My friends the Trees

Oh how I pity you now!
I saw that you were in love
And wished only to help you gaze on one another
But I am the Wind
And I know your limits
And I stopped blowing long ago
And the Water stopped shivering at that time too.
But still you are straining closer to the reflections made
by our friend the Sun
And the strain is caused by your vanity alone.
Love would lead you to a starved body
That could be nourished by the gaze of the other
Vanity would lead you to a well nourished broken
trunk."

Poem XX

All
That we have made
Is
Fantastic
And it all passes
And
You who
Hide
Your Hope
In trees
And
Your face
Behind clouds
Have allowed
Fear
To be
Placed
In eyes
Of men

Poem XXI

That
    Vile
Serpent
        Comes
    When
        I am
Sleeping
        And
    Fills
        My
    Heart
        With
    Venom

Poem XXII

A truth spoken into one ear
Shall rule them all

Poem XXIII

There are
No
Small differences
There is
No
Thin line
Between black and white

Poem XXIV

Light heart carries many burdens
Life starts merry many days
Burdens beat black waters against the hull
Light heart ferries dangers way

Poem XXV

Who pursued who?
I pursued her
Oh.
She had designs on me
Before I knew what was happening
She kissed me
I pursued her

Poem XXVI

I have been reminded
Who
I am
Life is to be
Not
So much spent
Planning
Who we want
To be
As men
As remembering
How we were
As
Children

Poem XXVII

I kiss you
Giggle
I kiss you
Wiggle

Poem XXVIII

And my right words are thrown back to me
Like dogs barking at a windmill

Poem XXIX

Gray days
In posh cafes
Black kids want to grow up to be Willie Mays
While the cities get built up like White dirty dishes on
trays
Like wishes that fade
Words that degrade
Are
All we
Remember

Poem XXX

He
Who questions his heart as the oracle
Will hear the hidden prophecy of a jealous god

He
Who questions his heart as his heart
Will hear the wind that will help him to stand

Poem XXXI

I stand barefoot
Hot mud between my toes
Friend and foe
Each take an arm
Holding me to the ground
I taste a pebble
I am bitterly reminded that I am one of many passing
along the shore

"Pebble"
We are the same
Though my time is shorter
To cross
My senses are outwitted
As are yours
Yet
Earnest and steadfast my spirit rises
The Tathagata calls me

Poem XXXII

My success will
Come
To me
While I snore
Come
To me
In a Dream
Not before
The Forgotten World
Where all comes and goes
Like the first snow
In flooded waters of spring

Poem XXXIII

Though
A man
May
Reach
His last day
Having built a
Pyramid
Of
Treasures
To
Not
Have grown
Simple kindness
In
Another heart
Hears
Failure

Poem XXXIV

Who
Really
Has known
Pleasurestreasures
Only woman?

Poem XXXV

Sometimes when I put on my shoes
I know
I can fly
Weightless
My toes will only flash to the
                                        ground
And strike
          like
          light

Then other times
I know
I shall only perform

Poem XXXVI

I
Should like
Very much
To
Know
The
Soft
Calling
Of the
Heart's whisper
From
The
Gentle
Harmonies
Of the
Siren

Poem XXXVII

Against
All words
Beats a
Loud
Wind
Dim
And
Holy
Moments
In
A
Chapel
Of a
Saint
Help me
To see
Myself
For what I am
A sham
An eater
Of man

Poem XXXVIII

There is no small distance between us and Paradise
Any such barrier
Would be
Insurmountable
No Harmony could exist
Before
Or
After
Such a boundary
If Peace exists
Inside ourselves
Then it must
Also
Exist
Outside ourselves
And
Our bodies
Are
Helpless
To prevent this Peace
Our bodies
Are not
To be
Mastered
It is our hearts we must reign

Poem XXXIX

Red China
What do I have to fear of you
You will sit back and watch
Like the clever suitor
Who escorts the young woman away
From the passionate brawl of potential lovers
And then you will win the Lady named Freedom
And I will lie
Stupid
Halfconscious
With my brothers
Knowing nothing good has come of our rage

Poem XL

Too-tut-ta
Did you see what the monkey saw?
He climbed up in a tree
Thought it would make him free
Make him free it did not
He is only as free as the tree
Too-tut-ta

Poem XLI

And the young boy
Smiled
Kissing the pink girl
While
Dirty playmates yelled
With disgust

And the young man
Smiled
Placing the ring on her white finger
While
Unwilling groomsmen felt friendship change

And the old men
Smiled
Raising their glasses to the lost leader
While
Tired hearts prepared
For final passage

Poem XLII

There are no heralds After the senses
Only before

There are no heralds Beyond the senses
Only before

Words line up in longlinesoflies we call sentences

There is no origin of Truth Past the senses
Only before

Each an oasis in this Country Desert
We have no need of sand so we cease to search
AfterBeyondPast

All that is before rests already in our grasp

Everything we seek Beyond this is merely conformity
with the world

Poem XLIII

There is no
Temptation
So
Great
As that
Of
The heart
I
Carry
Different faces
Everyday
When
I
Pray
I
Feel furthest from
God
And the Garden
He
Intended
For my leisure

Poem XLIV

Caine
Able
Cannables

Poem XLV

Only I can eat my dreams
Sharing my dreams
Is
Like
Asking someone else to chew my food

Poem XLVI

You who
Only
Think
Of
Yourself
In this world
What
Have you
To
Offer
But the refuse
From your gullet
Nothing
Impresses
So much
As
Servitude

Poem XLVII

I will become what I hate
I will ape what I hate
This is the inheritance ritual
Passed on through generations
I will grow quills
Nothing is unkind like circumstance

Poem XLVIII

Happiness or Sorrow
Where is our friendship stronger
Is the interim between our discussion
Longer
In happiness
And shall we say that this is bad
Or perhaps
Can we offer
That between two people who are comfortable with each
other
Silence forgives

Poem XLIX

All things in this life are passing
Even Love
We are more than capable of perverting
What should be eternal
I have no idea
What
It takes
To make
Or break
A man or his heart

Poem L

What
Is more
profane
Than the
Smallest
Stain
Or
Spot
On perfection